THE GHOSTLY TALES OF BISBEE

Published by Arcadia Children's Books
A Division of Arcadia Publishing
Charleston, SC
www.arcadiapublishing.com

First published 2022

Manufactured in the United States

ISBN 978-1-4671-9880-6

Library of Congress Control Number: 2022933024

All images courtesy of Shutterstock.com, pp. 34, 94 Paul R. Jones/Shutterstock.com

Spooky America

THE GHOSTLY TALES OF BISBEE

STACIA DEUTSCH

Adapted from *Haunted Bisbee* by Francine Powers

arcadia CHILDREN'S BOOKS

California
Arizona
New Mexic
Mexico
Pacific Ocean
Bisbee
1
2
3
4
5
6
7
8
9
10
11
12
13

Table of Contents & Map Key

Introduction

Have you ever been startled by a loud clang, but never figured out what made the sound? Have you smelled something like coffee, perfume, or a cigar when no one was around? Maybe you've seen a strange shadow in a dark room? Or heard voices when you were all alone?

Have you ever seen a ghost?

Francine Powers is a medium. That means that she can communicate with ghosts.

Growing up in the old mining town of Bisbee, Arizona, she'd heard stories that the town was haunted and then, when she was just six years old, she saw her first ghost.

Bisbee is a small town in Southeastern Arizona, just eleven miles from the Mexico border in Cochise County. About 5,000 people live there now, but back in the early 1900s there were double as many people. At that time, Bisbee was called the "Queen of Copper Camps" because it was a city founded by miners digging for fortune.

Some lucky prospectors made it rich and moved to fancy estates in newer, bigger cities.

The unlucky slunk away in the night, dreams dashed, without a nickel left to spend. And others, well, they decided to stay in

Bisbee. These early adventurers made a home for themselves and their families despite the summer heat and monsoon rainstorms.

Where once mining tents stood, they built permanent homes in Bisbee. As the city grew, people spread out from the city center, creating small neighborhood towns like Warren, Lowell, and San Jose. Miners needed supplies, places to stay, and entertainment. With each passing year, more businesses popped up in the area: hotels, restaurants, saloons, shops, and a railroad. It wasn't long before this busy, growing community needed schools, places to worship, and cemeteries.

Francine Powers was born nearly a hundred years after those first miners discovered copper in Bisbee. When she was six years old, she had her first ghostly sighting. Since that time, she's been an investigator, recording the history of her hometown and the stories told by Bisbee's ghosts. These are her stories.

If you don't believe in ghosts, read on.

The ghosts of Bisbee, Arizona have something to tell you . . . .

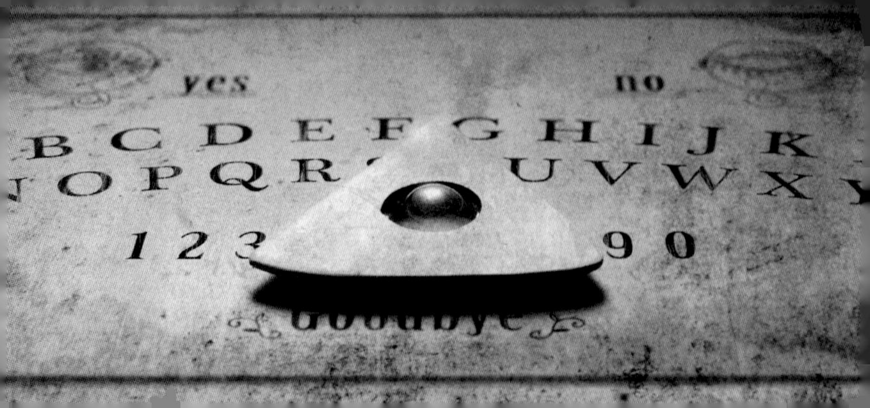
yes
no
B C D E F G H I J K
O P Q R U V W X
1 2 3 9 0

CHAPTER 1

The Haunted House on the Hill

About twenty-two miles outside of Bisbee, residents of Tombstone Canyon have reported ghostly sightings for decades. The name of the town—Tombstone Canyon—was never intended to draw in spirits. It's named that because the main road is the way to Tombstone, Arizona.

Francine Powers grew up in a Tombstone Canyon house built in 1928. Before her family moved in, they knew there had once been another building on the land. That old house had been torn down years earlier, but it had belonged to a miner and his wife. They had five children. The family only lived there a few years before moving away. But it seems they had such a connection to their old home, that in death, they all returned.

When she was six years old and in first grade, Francine's older sisters wanted to play a popular game. The Ouija Board consists of a panel with letters, numbers, and a little teardrop pointer. People would each ask a question and if a ghost was present, the spirit would guide the dial to spell a message. It was one of those kinds of games that was fun because it was also a little scary.

The game itself didn't reveal any ghosts. But soon after, strange things started happening in the house. Francine heard footsteps in the middle of the night. He sisters heard creaking floorboards in empty rooms. Lights flickered. One of the older sisters was watching TV. She saw a person's shadow reflected in the screen. When she turned to look, no one was there.

Francine's father heard a ball bouncing, He went to tell her, "No balls in the house." But Francine wasn't in the house!

Francine's mom found out about the Ouija game. She was a religious woman who believed that spirits should never be disturbed. In her opinion, the Ouija Board was to blame for the spirits in the house. She took the board outside and broke it in half.

The spirits didn't quiet down after that. In fact, Francine began to feel like a woman's spirit was often nearby. She was warm and comforting. The spirit sang in a pleasant voice. Francine could also feel her

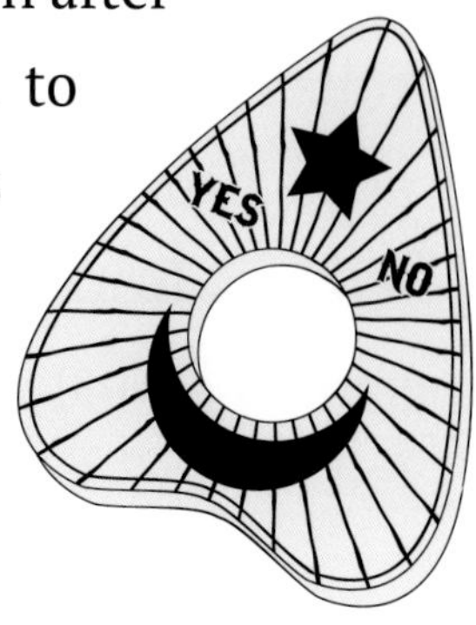

fear rise when a male spirit was nearby. He was angry and jealous. The man didn't only scare the woman, he scared young Francine.

Late one night, Francine woke up to see the shadow of a woman in her room. Startled, she called out to her sisters, which made the woman retreat. The ghost hid behind a lamp and didn't come out again until she was certain that she and Francine were alone.

Francine heard the ghost's footsteps on the wooden floor as she stepped out into a sliver of moonlight in the room. Her long hair was tied back in a tight knot, held by a large comb. She was wearing a long-sleeved blouse with a high collar. Her skirt draped to the floor. Laced up ankle boots peeked out as she walked. Francine felt no fear. The woman seemed kind and gentle. Perhaps this was the same spirit she'd felt before?

Francine relaxed a bit. Suddenly, the woman clasped her hands together tightly as if in prayer. Then, she bowed her head and sank, straight through the floorboards and out of sight.

Whenever she saw the ghostly woman, Francine wasn't afraid. But the male ghost gave her the chills. If he was around, the family dogs would bark. Once, there was the rough sound of tin cans being dragged around. Another time, it sounded like someone was having a fist fight in the attic. The whole family heard it and Francine's father went to investigate. He shouted up the steep stairs, but no one answered from the attic.

The next day, her parents called the local priest. They believed that religious leaders could push out spirits with prayers and holy water.

The priest came to the house and recited blessings in every room. He sprinkled holy water, chanted prayers for protection, and "released" the spirits that were trapped in the house.

It didn't work.

One afternoon, Francine's mother woke from a nap to find an eyeless face floating on the bedroom wall. She was terrified and asked the priest to come back.

A different priest came this time. The priest heard the fighting in the attic that Francine's family had heard before. He prayed as he went up the stairs. As he reached the top step, he crossed himself before opening the door. Francine watched the man's face go pale when he stepped into the room. The voices stopped.

The priest, thinking he quieted the spirits, turned

to leave. But the spirits were still there. They shoved the priest down the stairs. He crashed into the bottom wall and collapsed, unharmed but completely frightened.

After that, a formal exorcism was planned to rid the house of the ghostly spirits. It would take a professional to drive away evil spirits in the church's name. Often exorcists are called to remove spirits that have possessed people. But this time, they needed the ceremony to remove the spirits from the house.

The service began with a mass in the living room. It was believed that the floor heater served as some kind of vortex, a door, that allowed the spirits to come and go. The idea was to "close the vortex." As the priest began, Francine heard the ghostly woman singing, just like she'd done at their first meeting.

The priest carried a cross with the image of Jesus on it. The family followed him from room to room. He waved a silver staff and sprinkled holy water in each room.

The wind began to blow.

The windows vibrated.

A door slammed.

The family dogs howled uncontrollably.

And then, just as the house felt like it was swirling in a tornado of light, sound, and static electricity—it all stopped. The house went quiet and everything fell still.

Francine's parents believed that the spirits had finally left the house. But for Francine, who has felt ghostly presences her entire life, she knew the house on the hill was still haunted.

The ghosts are more subtle now. They live in the shadows and only appear in the background of photographs. Occasionally, a door bangs in an empty room.

Is Francine's family home haunted by the miner, his wife, and their children or someone else?

No one knows for sure. Francine believes that her sisters' game with the Ouija Board opened the living room vortex and it was never properly closed.

What do you think?

CAPTAIN

CHAPTER 2

Fear of Falling

Francine leads ghost-hunting tours of Bisbee and the surrounding towns. She has appeared on television shows, started her own online magazine, and has been interviewed for podcasts. Some of her ghost sightings were when she alone, but others happened when she was leading a group.

Imagine signing up for a tour, not sure what to expect, and having a ghostly spirit save your life! That's exactly what happened to a woman visiting Bisbee Fire Station Number 2.

The first station was built on Tombstone Canyon Road in 1914. It was a modern building for the time. The firemen had a room to stay in above the trucks. A pole let the firefighters swing down, fast, from the second floor, to get the horses and wagons whenever the emergency bell rang.

The building was renovated and changed through the years. But one thing remained the same. The firefighters that worked there reported that the place was haunted.

One day, Francine led a ghost hunting group to the fire house to investigate. There were a lot of stories of firefighters who had had served the community bravely. The ghosts could be any one of the men who had been there over the past hundred years.

In 1908, a deadly blaze tore through Bisbee's Main Street. A firefighter named George Marz inhaled acid fumes and died. Station Number 2 wasn't built yet. But was it possible that his spirit came to the new station and never left? George Marz was the only firefighter in the town's history to have died in the line of duty.

Or maybe the ghost was someone the firefighters tried to rescue but couldn't? There's no list of those names available.

No one knows for sure, but most people think that the ghost is a certain firefighter who died of a mysterious gunshot. The man wasn't at the Fire Station at the time he was shot. But he always joked that if he died, he would come back and haunt the station. He was a big prankster and this haunting might be his final joke.

Francine wrote down the stories she was told about ghostly encounters. Doors unlocked after they'd been shut for the night. The shower would go on when no one was around. Sometimes, there were wet footprints leading away from the bathroom. Pots and pans would jangle in the kitchen. Some witnesses even saw a faded apparition floating through walls.

Veteran firefighters like to play a trick on new team members. They would leave the new firefighter alone in the building, but not say anything about the ghost. New firefighters reported the sound of tools tinkering by the workstation or having the feeling that someone touched them when no one was there.

Curious that perhaps the ghost was in fact the prankster, Francine called out to the spirit, asking him to play a joke on two of the firefighters she'd met. Later, she heard that the two firefighters were walking into the main room when a lightbulb burst with a load crackling noise! The firefighters laughed, then told everyone about the ghost's big prank.

Years later, Francine went to the fire station with a tour group. She talked about the ghost and the pranks and told the firefighters' stories. The tour group was standing on a cement bridge that crossed a deep ditch in front of the building. One of the tourists decided to sit on an open part of the bridge's pipe fence. The woman felt wobbly and couldn't hold her balance. Just when it seemed that she might plummet into the deep ditch, something grabbed her, shoving her safely back onto the ground.

The woman believed with all her heart that it was the ghostly fireman. She told everyone, "He saved my life!"

CHAPTER 3

The Judge's Verdict

Francine was used to finding ghosts in Bisbee's oldest buildings. She wasn't surprised that when she went to work at the courthouse, the ghosts found her.

The Cochise County Superior Court-Bisbee Courthouse building was finished in 1931. It had been specially designed with a copper-plated roof and large bronze front doors. The lobby floor was made of beautiful imported marble. The front steps and arch leading into the building were impressive. It was a welcoming building to all visitors–living and dead.

The large, historic building wasn't only a place for judges to decide important cases. It also housed the community jail. The cells themselves were moved from an old courthouse in Tombstone, Arizona and brought to Bisbee. Were these old cells the source of the haunting that Francine experienced? She didn't know for sure. But when she had to go into the old cell area, the energy in the room made her uncomfortable.

A security guard named Hector said that he heard creepy voices and doors slamming when he was alone at night.

Some witnesses said it was a woman's spirit haunting the building, but others were certain that it was a man, specifically one of the first judges at the new courthouse.

John Wilson Ross was born in 1863 and became the first Cochise County superior judge at the new courthouse. He died in Pueblo, Colorado, but spent eleven years presiding over cases in the building. He'd also lived in town since about 1911, so it made sense that after he died, his spirit would want to return to the place he felt most comfortable.

Those who have seen him say that the ghost of Judge Ross looks exactly like the picture of him that hangs in the hallway. He is a wise man, weary with age—penetrating eyes and a stern expression. He is unmistakable when his apparition appears.

The judge has been seen in the Division 2 courtroom. In his old judge's chambers, the smell of smoke alerts visitors that the ghost is present. Witnesses have seen him walk the familiar path from the judge's bench back to that same chamber. Occasionally, he's also seen by the old jail area.

Perhaps he was also there, hidden in the shadows in the days that Francine was at work?

People who see the judge, say his ghost is not calm and comforting. Rather, that sense of unease that both Francine and the security guard reported follow him. He makes people nervous, edgy. They want to get as far away as possible.

A woman custodian was mopping a hallway late on evening when she noticed the judge lingering nearby. She stopped working, turned, and stared at the apparition. There was no doubt who stood before her. She'd passed by his photo a thousand times.

Judge Ross wore a 1940's era three-piece suit. He was wearing wire glasses. The custodian was scared. His eyes looked "crazy."

Her heart was racing when she turned away, not wanting to look at him even a second longer. When she was finally brave enough to look again, he was gone.

Judge Ross was not known to be a frightening person. He was one of the leading lawyers in Bisbee; he served on many committees and councils, and he ran for political office. It's possible that his presence in the building is frightening, not because he was a truly scary man, but rather because no one expects to see the judge still at work, years after his death.

CHAPTER 4

Spectral Scents

Ghostly apparitions aren't always seen—sometimes they are smelled.

The Loretto Academy—a Roman Catholic convent school—was once located behind the Bisbee Courthouse. The school was built in 1907. A year later, there were two hundred students from grades kindergarten to twelfth grade. The school's name was changed to the Saint Patrick's School and closed in the early

1970s. But the building was never vacant. A solitary nun has lived there ever since she died.

For decades, students avoided the downstairs bathroom. The story was passed student to student, grade to grade, that an elder nun was seen hovering around. It was said that she wore a long black floor-length gown and the traditional habit of a Catholic nun. Some saw her appear in mirrors, fogging the glass. Others said she would turn on the water faucets in the bathroom. But the common thing among nearly everyone who saw the ghostly nun was the smell of coffee.

Have you ever smelled something that is out of place? Perfume is common. Cigars too. Coffee is another scent associated with ghosts. When you smell things that aren't there, it's called an olfactory hallucination or phantosmia. Some think it's a medical disorder. Or maybe it's a memory? But for those who have smelled coffee in the Loretto Academy, they were certain a ghost is nearby.

So who was she?

That is the mystery. No one has spoken to the nun, though many people have seen her.

It's thought that the nuns that worked in the school had their own building nearby on Taylor Avenue. That's where they lived before the nuns were moved to a more modern home directly across from the academy. This nun, judging by how long sightings have been reported, may have come from the Taylor Avenue house.

Why is she still haunting the school? Although the school closed fifty years ago, the nun seems to have stayed behind. Maybe she is hopeful that someday some students will come back, or perhaps she longs for happier days. No one knows. The Loretto School building is still standing. If you visit, beware of the basement!

The Fair Store, Bisbee

CHAPTER 5

The Fair Store Séance

In 1908, there was a tragic fire along Main Street in the heart of Bisbee. The fire started in The Grand Hotel and swept through the businesses and local residences. It was the largest fire ever recorded for the town, causing a lot of damage. It took three hours to put out the blaze. More than 500 people lost their homes. Luckily, no one died. But that doesn't mean the area isn't haunted by ghosts who were there on that tragic day.

Sam and Ben Frankenberg owned a department store a few doors down from the Grand Hotel. Sam Frankenberg noticed the fire burning before it spread to all the neighboring businesses. At the time, he told the newspaper that he could have stopped the fire with a garden hose–but he didn't have one. Neither, it turned out, did anyone else. The fire quickly consumed building after building until the street was mostly ash.

The Frankenberg store—called the Fair Store—had been an elegant place. It was staffed with expert employees from big cities like Detroit and New York. They carried men's and women's clothing, hats, and shoes in all the latest fashions. Fancy carpets for the home. So many nice things to buy!

Imagine how lovely the store must have been, and such a wonderful place to spend an afternoon. After the fire, the store was rebuilt and stayed in business until 1928. After that, the building was used for a variety of businesses. In 1968, it was donated to the Restoration Council of Bisbee and turned into a museum.

The volunteers at the museum knew about the ghost. Some had seen her wandering the second floor. Others said they heard her speaking softly but couldn't make out the words.

Was she a shopper who loved the store and decided to make it her haunt? An employee perhaps? Had she wandered there before the fire? Or had she come later, after the store was re-built?

There was only one way to find out.

Francine arranged a séance. A séance is a meeting where someone tries to communicate with the dead. As a medium, Francine was an expert in such meetings. She gathered a few ghost hunters to see if they could reach out to the ghost. It was Francine's birthday when they met late at night in the museum.

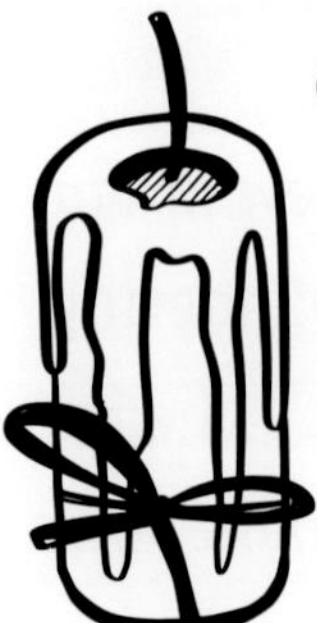

The three ghost hunters sat in chairs on the mezzanine between the first and second floors. The lights were off and the room was dark and quiet. She instructed the spirit to tap something if they were there.

The ghost hunters were excited when they heard tapping from a nearby display of old sewing machines. They told the ghost what to do: after a question, tap once for yes. Silence meant no.

The ghost hunters recited the alphabet. The ghost tapped each time they reached a letter in her name. E? Tap. F? No. L? Tap.

Her name was Elaina.

"Did you work in the Fair Store?"

Tap.

That meant she had worked there!

Shop girl?

Nothing.

Clerk? Saleslady?

Silence.

Seamstress?

Tap.

They asked if she recognized anyone in

the room. She "knew" the museum staff, but not Francine.

They asked if she knew Ben Frankenberg. She tapped yes. She also told them she wasn't living alone in the building. Her son was there, too.

A few more questions revealed that she was in her thirties and had brought her son to work with her at the store. She confessed that her son liked to play tricks on the museum staff by moving things around.

Spirits who communicate with the living get tired easily. Soon, she stopped answering the questions. The ghost hunters were happy with the progress they'd made and sat quietly taking in the moment. That was when they all heard the quick steps on the floor above them. They didn't know if Elaina had moved to the floor above, or if there was another spirit present. The communication stopped.

Francine led three séances at the store. Elaina retuned each time. She answered questions and made noises to let the guests know she was there.

Her son continues to play tricks on the employees at the museum.

The Fair Store was a lovely place to work, before and after the fire. For Elaina and her son, it remains a lovely place to haunt.

CHAPTER 6

Jailhouse Jitters

The county jail on OK Street was overcrowded and filthy. Built in 1905, it was close to the saloons and nightlife on Brewery Gulch, a popular entertainment area of town. By 1915, the cells were packed nightly, usually with people who had had a bit too much rowdy fun down at the bars.

It was hot, sweaty, and the conditions were miserable. Prisoners complained. People were getting sick from the conditions.

The jail couldn't hold enough prisoners. The town needed a new jail. When the prisoners were finally moved, the OK Street building sat vacant for years. Then, in 1974, a famous actor decided he wanted it.

John Wayne was known for his western movies, many set around the town of Bisbee. He and his business partner, Edwin J. Smart, bought the building. It was rumored that his intention was to restore it and turn it into a John Wayne Museum, a tribute to the actor's career. John Wayne was going to donate his own memorabilia. He had a large collection of guns, costumes, framed photos, and other items. As time passed, it was clear that the museum plans weren't going to happen and the building stayed empty. Except for the ghosts.

This historic site is a now hotbed of paranormal activity and a thriving hotel for those who want to sleep with spirits. It's called the OK Street Jailhouse Inn.

While on a group tour, Francine met two people who had just stayed there overnight. One of the men said that he'd woken early and gone to the kitchen to make coffee. He felt like someone was following him down the stairs. But as soon as he reached the ground level the feeling disappeared. His friend then woke up thinking someone was pressing a hand on his forehead. No one was there.

Another time, a guest reported that they'd heard crying on the second floor. It seemed to be coming from the closet.

Others who have stayed at the OK Street Jailhouse Inn, have their own stories to tell. They say they felt like someone was watching them. It's always reported that the ghosts in the building carry feelings of anger or sadness.

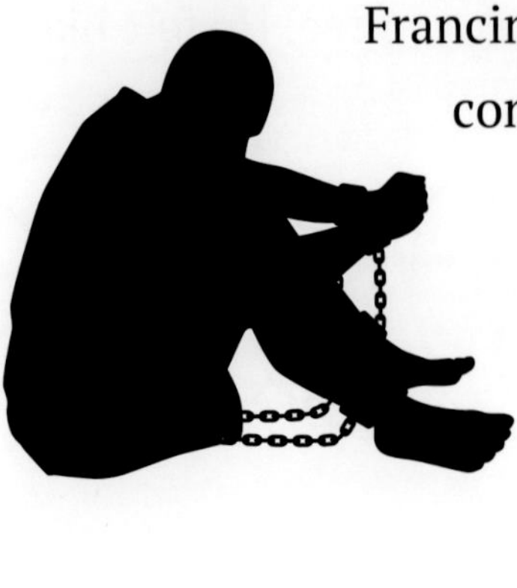

Francine has tried to make contact with the jail ghosts. On the second floor, she took photos that appear to have light orbs floating in them. If each of the orbs represent a single spirit, there are more than fifty souls haunting the old jail.

Anyone can stay overnight at the Jailhouse Inn.

Are you brave enough?

CHAPTER 7

Spook-Land

Reporters are known for their dedication to facts, but sometimes the facts are so strange that there is no obvious explanation. In October of 1909, the journalists at the *Bisbee Daily Review* wrote about a ghost living in Zacatecas Canyon. The article quoted Constable Parley McRae, who insisted there were no ghosts. He guessed that an unknown troublemaker was living in the hills. But for who felt the wrath of the ghost—called the "Woman in White"—there was no doubt. She existed and she was angry.

Near the beginning of 1909, the local constable had discovered a child's body in the mountains. Authorities investigated, desperate to discover who might have left the body there without a proper burial. But they couldn't find the answer. That same night, rocks showered down on the canyon village for the first time.

Neighbors complained that in the hours before midnight, huge boulders crashed down the hills towards their homes below. Some of these rocks were big enough to dent doors and cause damage to homes. Police went out to the area each time someone called, hoping to arrest a person causing the problems.

Night after night, the police found nothing. They could only guess that whoever the troublemaker was, they could move around the brushy hills quickly. The police couldn't find them.

A week later, the rock-throwing suddenly stopped. The valley was once again calm. The police ended their investigation. But the quiet didn't last. Shortly after, people began seeing a woman appear in the spot that the child's body was found. She'd weep, covering her face with her hands, and cry in heartbreaking heaves. The woman would sit there for about an hour, giving people from the village time to rush up the hill, hoping to find out who she was. But when anyone approached, she'd disappear. Some people tried to chase her, but they could never catch up.

The sightings stopped a few months later and again, the canyon was quiet. Like before, the quiet didn't last.

One night, a drunken woodcutter was shooting his gun and accidentally hit some dynamite sticks. The dynamite exploded, blowing up a house where a woman lived. She tragically died. After that, ghostly sightings began again.

The police were called about rocks being tossed down on the homes. Boulders being pushed from the hills. One home was so badly damaged that the people had to move away.

Was the ghost the woman who was accidentally killed? Or had the old ghost returned?

The ghostly figure revealed herself to the village, appearing at the top of a hill. Like before, she wore white. But which woman was she? No one knew for sure. She'd stand there for a long minute or two, then begin to cry—loud sobs—before disappearing.

In her sorrow, she seemed to glow. Her cries made everyone who heard them feel drawn into her sadness. Her moans echoed through the valley.

For a while, the ghost appeared every night after the woman was accidentally killed. People were afraid to go outside at night. Some people carried guns, thinking they could protect themselves or their families from the spirit. A few gun owners would shoot in the direction of the spirit, as if that might scare her off.

Police officers were called to investigate. While they were in the hills, the usual activity seemed to get worse. Handfuls of small rocks would fly at the officers, as if thrown by a mighty force.

None of the men who came to search for the ghost reported seeing her. The officers, led by Constable McRae, declared firmly that there was no ghost. They thought maybe people from a neighboring village were causing mischief. The residents insisted they were haunted by "La Spiritu," but the formal report was there was nothing unusual in Zacatecas Canyon.

The newspaper report in 1909 raised the possibility that a ghost was living in the canyon hills. A hundred years later, Francine still heard stories about "La Spiritu."

Francine knew that people reported that

rocks were randomly thrown at homes and people on hiking trails. Strange tracks were often seen near the place where the rocks originated. The tracks appeared to be hooves, but in pairs, not in sets of four. Not human feet, as one might expect.

A local woman told Francine that she was once bombarded with pieces of burning ember when she was in the valley. She looked for a large, nearby fire, but the only flames she saw were the ones that floated by her. They disappeared as quickly as they had appeared.

Another woman, who'd lived her whole life in Bisbee, said that when she was a child, asleep in her bedroom, she often heard a woman's unnatural scream. It didn't seem human. The wailing woke her, but also seemed far enough away that she didn't feel unsafe. She'd close her eyes tightly and wait a few minutes, then the cries would fade away.

Francine experienced something strange in Zacatecas Canyon, too. When she was giving a tour to a group of people interested in the hauntings of the valley, rocks were thrown at the golf cart she was driving.

A member of the tour asked if she set it up. She hadn't. Suddenly, a rock was thrown

directly at Francine's head! The guests were scared. Francine hurried them away from the area.

Another night, she was with a group and they all heard a strange sound. It wasn't a person, but it didn't seem like an animal either. Whatever it was, the voice was low and raspy. A woman on the tour begged them to leave quickly. Francine agreed. They drove away.

The ghost of the Zacatecas Valley has haunted the area for over a hundred years. No one knows who she is, but if you are driving or hiking nearby, be sure to watch for rocks!

CHAPTER 8

Louis Maure's Ghost

Brewery Gulch is an area of Bisbee where Zacatecas Canyon meets Brewery Avenue. Here, in Upper Brewery Gulch, houses were built near one another. It was a friendly neighborhood, where people gathered and everyone knew one another. It is in one of these homes that our story begins . . .

In the early 1900's, Louis Maure lived in Upper Brewery Gulch. His lovely stone house had four bedrooms. He liked the area and he liked the house. So much, in fact, that even after his brutal death, Louis continued to live in his home.

His death certificate reveals a lot of information. He was thirty years old. French American. Single. He died because of a fracture at the base of his skull.

Residents of the area believed that Louis was killed by robbers. Like many Bisbee miners at the time, he came home late after a long shift at work. It would have been about 1:00 am, when he reached his block and was approached by five men. As he got closer, he saw that one of the men was injured and the others were carrying him down the street.

What Louis didn't know, was that this same group had just attempted to rob his neighbor, James McDonald. James McDonald had shot and injured the man who was being carried.

Louis didn't know the whole situation. But the theory is that he recognized one of the other men in the gang. They were scared he'd turn them in once he heard what had happened. They attacked Louis Maure with rocks and sticks. Louis lived a few hours after the attack but was unconscious the whole time. He never identified the men who killed him.

Still, all five men were caught and sent to prison in Yuma, Arizona, for attempted robbery. They were never prosecuted for killing Louis Maure.

Louis Maure knew who killed him. His soul couldn't rest because the men had, in his eyes, gone unpunished. His ghost returned to his home where it paced, angry and frustrated, scaring off anyone who tried to live there.

Justice Owen Murphy bought the house after Louis Maure's death. He rented it to others. Renters would report unearthly groans echoing through the rooms. They saw invisible entities walking through locked doors. The sound of footsteps echoed in the hallways. Lights flickered.

Families would move in, then move right out again. In a short span of time, six different families tried living there, only to be chased away by Louis Maure's angry ghost.

The tiny stone house became famous throughout the neighborhood because it was haunted.

Would you dare to live in Louis Maure's home?

CHAPTER 9

Which Ghost Haunts the Wills House?

Francine took her Haunted Historical Cart Tour guests to the old Wills House in Upper Brewery Gulch because ghosts were often seen hanging around this old residence and the apartments next to it.

George B. Wills built three recycled brick Victorian buildings around 1902. They were divided into apartments—some in the Wills family residence, as well as in the other buildings. The last building had five rooms for rent. It was smaller than the others—only one-story high.

Thomas Constable was an Englishman and a long-time resident in one of the apartments in the last building. He raised Greyhound dogs and had a reputation for chasing away neighborhood children who came too close.

The most likely souls that remain in these buildings are either George B. Wills or Thomas Constable.

When Francine took her tours to the apartments, they were never surprised to find a glowing human figure standing between the two tallest buildings. The strange thing was that he never appeared to the naked eye—only in photos. It was as if they could only catch him when he was peeking around one of the buildings, staring out at the tour group.

If you were a detective, would you think this ghost was George B. Wills because it was closest to the apartment building where he lived? Perhaps, but let's investigate further.

Tour groups occasionally heard footsteps across the porch of the one-story building. If they pointed a flashlight at the porch, glowing orbs were caught in pictures of the small front yard where Thomas Constable would walk his dogs.

Once, Francine was leading a group of ghost hunters around the apartments, which were being renovated by new owners. They went inside one of the buildings. There, one of the ghost hunters began to communicate with

a male entity. The group went outside and the ghost followed them into a small yard. She asked the spirit his name, but he didn't say. Rather, the ghost murmured that he was "proud of this place."

The ghost hunter asked if the spirit liked the new plans and renovations.

He answered, "Yes."

She asked the spirit to make a noise, since the others couldn't hear his voice like she could.

A rock hit the roof.

The ghost disappeared after that.

So, who is haunting the apartments in Upper Brewery Gulch? Is it George B. Wills? It might make sense that he was proud of the buildings he created so he decided to stay in death. Is the ghost Thomas Constable, still protecting his home?

CHAPTER 10

Playing in the Cemetery

Ghosts sometimes welcome kids to the park that used to be a cemetery.

Bisbee's first cemetery was created sometime in the 1880's. It wasn't long before the old plots were neglected, and tombstones were tipping over. No one was taking care of the area. Mining families often didn't stay long in Bisbee and there was no one around to tend to family graves. Children loved to hide among the tilted stones and run through the weeds. That gave the community an idea.

In 1913, a plan was created to turn the old cemetery into a city park. Moving a cemetery is not an easy project. But before grass and playground equipment could be brought in, the bodies had to be relocated. The law said that the remains of anyone buried there had to be taken to another cemetery or suitable place

and that the city had to pay for it. The law also said that all monuments and gravestones had to be moved and put at the new cemetery as well.

It was decided. A list was created, with every grave assigned a name and a number. The people who had been buried and their tombstones would move together to a new site in Lowell, Arizona. Sounds easy, right?

The removal of the bodies began in January 1915. Things did not go as smoothly as planned. The names of the dead were written haphazardly in pencil on various pieces of paper, not in a single logbook. Of

the thirty-four bodies removed and relocated, twenty-three were identified, the rest were labeled "unknown." Some information was also mis-recorded. Birthdates and grave sites were not written down correctly.

Local residents were concerned that the company that moved the bodies were not careful and might have left some graves behind. The company promised they removed them all. Construction on the new city park began.

City Park was dedicated in May 1916. The Arizona Governor even came to the celebration. The park was more than a playground. It had space for political meetings and speeches, ceremonies, and neighborhood dances. There was a band shell created for concerts.

After the park was finished, one resident said that she would never attend anything in the City Park because she didn't want to "dance on the dead."

When Francine was in junior high school, she lived in a house nearby. The entrance has seventy-five steps. One day when she was visiting, Francine met a young boy-ghost. She didn't get a bad feeling from him, rather he seemed sad. He hung out near some trash cans. They never spoke.

She also saw a young man-ghost in the park. He pointed to a space where his mother's grave used to be. When they spoke, he told her that the ground was special and not a place for children to play.

In 2004, there was a ghost-hunting workshop in Bisbee. After hearing Francine's stories, one of the ghost hunters said that

years ago, she'd had a strange experience in the park as well. She was just entering when a cold, spine-chilling, breeze swept through her. She immediately felt nauseous and a little dizzy. Days later, whenever she looked in a mirror, a young boy would be there, shadowing her reflection. The boy had since disappeared and now, she wanted to go back to the park.

They went together, along with another woman. Francine stood where she had once sensed the boy's presence. The ghost hunter was surprised to discover that was the same place she'd felt the chill! The woman took a long twig from a nearby tree and stuck it into the ground. They were going to have a séance and see if they could communicate with the boy.

If the boy was present, he could move the stick to answer the questions. They videotaped the séance.

Did he remember Francine?

Yes. The twig moved.

They counted from one to fourteen.

The twig moved at twelve. (He was twelve years old.)

Was his mother buried in the old cemetery there?

Yes.

Was she still there?

Yes. (Perhaps all the bodies hadn't been moved after all?)

Was he protecting her?

Yes.

Did he want to leave the park?

No.

After a while, he stopped moving the twig. Either he vanished or became too tired to communicate any more.

On the haunted tour, Francine took many people to City Park. Francine doesn't think the boy's mother was still in the park. More likely, the boy didn't know his mother was moved. He haunts the site where he believes she is buried.

And still, Francine has had other ghostly experiences in the same area. Once, she was speaking when the large bow on her jacket was untied by invisible hands. Another time, she saw a ghostly figure standing nearby when no one was there. It seems that the moment

she steps into the park, a ghost usually joins her. Just in case someone wants to follow her home, like the boy did with her ghost hunter friend, Francine tells the ghosts in a clear, strong voice, "You don't have permission to follow me." She reminds her guests to tell the ghosts the same message.

If you make it clear to a ghost that they cannot follow you, they won't.

That's some very good advice!

CHAPTER 11

The Fortune Teller

Today, the only thing marking the spot of the Hermitage Saloon is a tile in the sidewalk. If we could go back to the early 1900s, we'd see that the saloon was a popular hotspot. The two-story building had a summer garden upstairs, while the beer hall was downstairs. The Hermitage had a first-rate soda fountain, plus, they sold imported chesses and meats. It was a fun place to hang out with friends, and if you wanted, to also bet on sports.

After 1920, when selling alcohol was illegal, the upstairs area was converted to a gym, while sodas continued to be sold downstairs. The businesses of the Hermitage adapted to the times and many people stopped by when they were in Bisbee. Throughout the years, it was a booming business, regardless of the Prophecy of Doom. What's that, you ask?

In 1909, a fortune-teller predicted that a fire would destroy not only the saloon, but all of Brewery Gulch sometime that year. People were on alert and careful. Fire didn't happen in 1909. But just as people were relaxing, calling the prophecy a hoax, a fire really did break out. In 1911, a small explosion across the street from the Hermitage started a blaze.

The fire began when a giant tamale pot, heated on a gasoline stove, burst into flames.

The flames were so large, they spread quickly across the street. A shoeshine stand outside the saloon caught fire. The Reserve Fire Chief rushed into the saloon and grabbed a bottle of seltzer water from the Hermitage bar. He thought he'd put out the flames, but hot sparks were in the cash drawer of the shoeshine station, and the fire set a shoeshining brush alight. More seltzer put out the fire. When it was finally extinguished, people began to relax once more. The fortune-teller couldn't have meant a fire that small, right?

Two years later, in 1913, a larger fire broke out one evening. The roof of the Tovres and Co. meat market had defective wiring. For fifteen minutes, firefighters evacuated the area and fought the flames.

The fire engulfed the entire wooden roof. Had it not been for two visitors from New York, the building would have been overcome and perhaps, the Hermitage with it. The men sounded an alarm, searched for anyone inside the meat market, and saved the day. The Hermitage had a scorched wall, but not other damage.

Once again, people began to relax. The fortune-teller's prediction was mostly forgotten.

Decades passed. In 1976, the Hermitage Building was no longer a saloon, but instead was being used by the *Brewery Gulch Gazette*, a small newspaper. On May 12, a fire was started by an arsonist. No one was hurt, but the printing press, printing supplies and historic photos all were destroyed. By the time the flames were put out, the historic Hermitage Saloon building was burned to the ground.

This terrible fire took place sixty-seven years after the fortune-teller's dooming prediction. Do you think she might have been able to know the future? Or was it simply a coincidence?

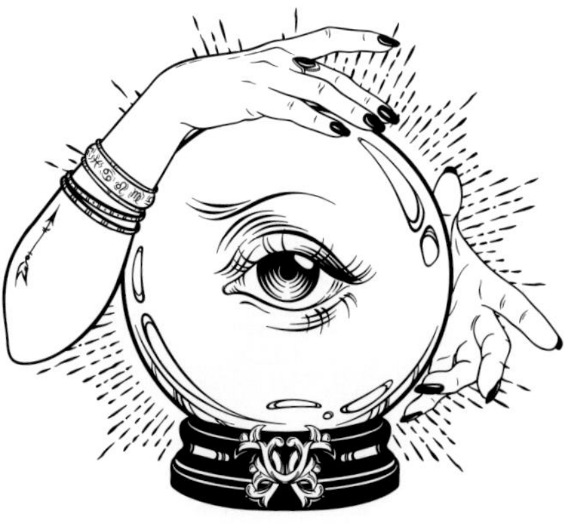

CHAPTER 12

School House Inn

At the top of Tombstone Canyon, there was a school. For nearly two decades, elementary students attended it from first to fourth grade. It was built in 1918, and as the years went by and other schools opened. The old building found new purpose. Now, it is a nine-room bed and breakfast called the School House Inn. If you choose to stay at the inn, it's important to know, the building is haunted.

The schoolhouse has always had reports of paranormal activity. In recent years, those reports seem to be intensifying.

The owners of the Inn decided to decorate the hotel with antique toys to go along with the schoolhouse theme. One of those owners, Paula Roth, said that when she works to set up rooms for new guests, she passes old doll buggies they placed in the hallway. A particular carriage, with a vintage doll inside, was pushed out from the wall one day, and nearly tripped her as she carried a load of sheets. The floors are flat and she didn't see another reason that the buggy might move–except if a ghost moved it.

Another time, a guest at the inn went downstairs

at two in the morning to get a cup of tea. He was staying in the school's old Geography classroom. As he returned to his room, he heard children giggling in the otherwise empty hallway.

In the Arithmetic Suite, a spirit wearing a long flowing gown from the 1880's appeared. The guest reported that when she was settling in to sleep, the woman revealed herself and was levitating around, as if looking for something. After a few moments, she disappeared through a wall.

A man who stayed in the History Room said that while he was sleeping, someone tugged and pushed at his leg. He woke up, but no one was there. When he tried to fall back asleep, it happened again. He was scared.

Another visitor in the History Room said that a music box, left for decoration, began to play. He hadn't touched it.

John Lambert, the Inn's late co-owner, had ghostly experiences as well. His apartment was at the end of a long hallway. He once saw a shadow go past. He checked, but it wasn't the other owner, Paula Roth, and none of the rooms were booked. The shadow went back and forth a few more times, but he never made contact.

In the old Writing Room, Paula Roth noted that after she made up the bed, she turned to find the impression of a body in the covers.

Francine also had a strange experience at the School House Inn Bed and Breakfast. She was there taking photos. As she stood at the end of the hallway, looking through the camera on her phone, she could see a white ball was following another guest. The ball moved with the man and appeared in every picture she took.

Are these ghostly adults that haunt the building? Spirits of kids from the school? Who could it be?!

The Inn at Castle Rock

CHAPTER 13

The Inn at Castle Rock

The Inn at Castle Rock sits where Tombstone Canyon Road turns into Main Street in Bisbee. The Inn was first known as the Muirhead House, built in 1895, as a rest place for miners.

The boarding house was built by a man who knew the needs of miners, because he was one himself. Joseph J Muirhead came to town to work at the Copper Queen Mining Company. As he earned money in the mines, he saved and eventually bought the house. Muirhead also became Bisbee's first elected mayor. He was devoted to the town and the people who lived there.

Muirhead died in 1930. After that, his wife took over running the boarding house. For another 18 years, she managed the place. It was on a quiet afternoon that Catherine Jane Muirhead had an unexpected guest join the hotel registry: Mable Watters.

In October 1935, Mable Watters died.

She was thirty-four years old when she was simply walking up the street near the hotel when tragedy happened. Mable's two children and husband were not with her.

As it happened, Mable Watters was on the sidewalk at the exact moment that Norman Duke was cleaning his gun across the street. Norman was a miner at the Copper Queen. He was standing in a window, facing the street, when the gun accidentally fired. The bullet went through the window and hit Mable. She died instantly.

Norman Duke told police he was cleaning the gun, getting ready to go deer hunting, and didn't realize it was loaded. The investigators declared the death an accident and the case was dropped.

And yet, Mable was not at peace.

Catherine Muirhead sold the boarding house and it became apartments. Then later, the building was restored to an inn with fourteen rooms.

Throughout the changes to the building, Mable has remained present. People have reported seeing the apparition of a slim woman wearing all black wandering along the sidewalk across from the Inn. Guests in the hotel say they've seen Mable Watters roaming from room to room. Some say it feels as though she is looking for someone.

Mable never knew that it was Norman Duke who shot her that day. She didn't know where the bullet had come from. Her death was sudden and surprising. Could it be that her ghost is searching for the answers?

It is said that Mable Watters won't rest until she knows who killed her.

CHAPTER 14

The Headless Miner

Bisbee had more than fifty mines and two open pits during the boom years. There is one deep shaft that goes down to about 3,300 feet. This is called the Lowell Shaft, and since the early 1900's, it's been the most talked about mine because of the legendary incident that happened there.

A miner, working in the shaft saw another miner laying on top of a pile of timber. This was unusual. Had the man gone for a nap? The miner went to touch the man. He was going to ask if he was okay. The man didn't move, so the miner went to help him sit up. As he raised the man to seating, the miner realized the body didn't have a head!

The miner's terrified screams shook the caverns. He dropped the headless man back onto the lumber pile and raced from the shaft. He didn't stop running until he was safely home.

After that, the headless miner was seen at another shaft by other miners. Those men didn't run, rather they looked away and kept on working.

Rumors about the ghost spread from mine to mine. Some miners believed the headless ghost existed, while others thought it was a joke. For those who believed, they were nervous about being left alone in dark places and were jumpy at any little noise. Some brave miners even wanted to meet the ghost and went looking for him.

It's not known how many miners saw the headless ghost, but everyone had a theory. The *Bisbee Evening Miner* newspaper even did an article about the headless miner in 1909.

If this was a legend in your town, would you go searching for the headless miner? Or would you stay far, far away?

Conclusion

Francine is gentle with the ghosts she meets. She hopes that they can share their stories and allow her, as a medium, to relay that information to the world.

Bisbee, Arizona, is a historic community where most of the ghosts are happy to welcome visitors. If you are there, you can let the ghosts guide you to see the city as they remember it.

Now you know where to find them. Do you dare to seek out the Ghosts of Bisbee, Arizona?

New York Times Best Selling author **Stacia Deutsch** has written more than three hundred children's books including The Jessie Files, a spin off of the beloved Boxcar Children mystery series. Stacia lives in Temecula, California, where she is member of the historical society and loves hearing spooky stories! Find her at www.staciadeutsch.com. Instagram @staciadeutsch_writes and www.facebook/staciadeutsch.

Check out some of the other Spooky America titles available now!

Spooky America was adapted from the creeptastic Haunted America series for adults. Haunted America explores historical haunts in cities and regions across America. Each book chronicles both the widely known and less-familiar history behind local ghosts and other unexplained mysteries. Here's more from *Haunted Bisbee* author Francine Powers: